The Music Maker

Liz Kershaw

First Published in the UK in 2018 by Mantle Arts

Copyright © Liz Kershaw 2018

The right of Liz Kershaw to be identified as author
of this work has been asserted by her.

ISBN 978-1-9998416-1-4

Mantle Lane Press
Springboard Centre
Mantle Lane
Coalville
LE67 3DW
www.mantlelanepress.co.uk
www.mantlearts.org.uk

Printed and bound in the UK by
Imprint Digital, Upton Pyne, Exeter, EX5 5HY

Cover illustration by Jessamy Hawke
www.jessamyhawke.co.uk

To Neil, for all his love and support.

Contents

Prologue.

I was not to blame for what happened to Stella. After all, I was dealing with some powerful forces: my own and Stella's fallible humanity, and Kai, such a clever hunter, whose precise nature defies definition still, two years on, and probably always will.

It was not my fault. At least, that's what I believe on weekdays, when I'm busy at work in the cool white space of my laboratory, and my thoughts are ordered and neat. But, there are times, if I wake in the creeping hours of darkness, when I wonder if I could have done more to protect Stella after I became wary of Kai's true nature, and what he might be planning. I've had experience of others' malign intentions and it has made me careful. Poor Stella had nothing but a naïve faith that no one would hurt her because she was good.

At such times, I lie in bed too chilled to sleep and guilt creeps in to torment me. The solitude of night helps my memory to play tricks: I see a man's form in the shadows on the landing, I hear an echo of Kai's dangerous music in the rush of the wind. I feel Stella's cold breath in the draught from the window as it grazes my cheek, and whispers, "Will you help me to come back?"

But then, these are nightmare fancies which I'm able to banish when the morning comes and sanity dawns with the daylight. The part I played was minor, and to be fair, even that was directed by Kai. Perhaps I did all I could, and, in the end, Stella was the mistress of her own fate as I am mistress of mine. She could have listened to my warnings; she had the chance to turn away and yet, she carried on.

How can I be blamed if she made a deliberate decision to fall?

1

*A wondrous thing of our dreaming
Unearthly, impossible seeming…*

No one noticed the man enter the cathedral. It was a Wednesday night in late November, and we were rehearsing Elgar's *The Music Makers* for our end-of-year performance, sixty or so singers grouped together in the space under the soaring Gothic tower. The gale outside howled and raged against the windows, the volume of our singing rose to compensate, and we became lost to everything apart from the intensity of the music. Was that how he slipped in, unseen? I thought so then, but I came to wonder later whether he might have blown in as dust through the gaps around the panes and materialised in the dark hinterland behind the altar. How else to explain how a man could walk through that vast echo chamber of a building without his boots striking on the brasses, or the west door grinding against the flagstones?

We had a short break after the first run through and then, as the great bourdon bell struck the eighth hour, Anthony called us to order, raised his baton, and flicked his hand to count us in to go again from the top.

That was the moment that my life changed, and Stella's tilted into free-fall, although we had no idea of that until much later when the damage had been done. All we knew then, all we could be aware of in that first moment, was that a man, invisible in the shadows beyond the lanterns, began to sing.

"We are the music makers,
And we are the dreamers of dreams,
Wand'ring by lone sea-breakers,
And sitting by desolate streams;"

There is an elemental power in a choir. Many bodies merge into one spirit in a blending of heartbeats and breathing that takes possession of each individual for as long as the music lasts. We consent to this control and we relish the feeling it brings: the tingle in the spine, the quick thrilling rush of heat as a song pulses through from chest to limbs. This man's voice did not seek consent – it launched an invasion and stormed in. I had barely a moment to register the sound of it, strong and sweet and true, before it flooded me, forced everything but awareness of his presence from my mind and reduced me to nothing but a shell of skin and bone no longer filled with my thoughts or will, only his.

Looking back, I can see how clever he was. How he'd somehow scented out those qualities in Stella that marked her as prey and tracked her to our choir, searching for anything in any one of us that he could turn to his advantage in winning her. A hint of darkness or spite, a chink that might allow his malevolence to find its way in.

He struck lucky with me. I have a trace of frost in my blood, or so I've been told. It's proved useful in my job: all those experiments when I've changed an organism's environment and stood by dispassionately, observing it struggle to survive. I've found a pleasure in this work which I'd never dare confess to others; I've always hidden it behind a regretful sigh and the general catch-all: "It's important medical research". But he found me out in those few moments of communion, saw right to the centre of me and chose me because of it.

> *"Yet we are the movers and shakers*
> *Of the world, for ever, it seems."*

At the end of the first stanza, he stopped singing. Anthony's baton stalled, the organ faded. I felt a twist, inside, cold as an ice chip, that sent a shiver through me and raised the hairs from my skin. And then, as that unearthly voice withdrew from its possession of me, my chest heaved with sudden loss and loneliness and I was left chilled, as if I'd been tumbled naked into biting, bright lit air.

Stella, beside me, made a noise, a breathy little gasp. Her lips were apart and her small mouth hung slightly open; she seemed distressed at its betrayal and moved her hand up to her chin as if to close it. The women around us appeared variously stunned: blanched, wide-eyed. One of the sopranos had slumped into a chair. Another's hands were shaking. After a minute or two, I recovered my equilibrium sufficiently to look behind me, and seek out the stranger.

We always rehearsed in front of the wide steps at the altar end of the nave; concert formation: four blocks in a shallow semi-circle: soprano, alto, tenor, bass. The singer had stepped back, away into the dim space between the unlit choir stalls beyond us, and was hard to make out in the shadows before the altar. Behind him, the east window arched up to the vaulted ceiling, blank and colourless until the wind outside forced clouds away from the moon, and bleached light shone in through the ruby and green stained-glass. I could see a man framed by it, featureless and unknowable; all I could gather of him was an impression of height, and breadth and presence.

Anthony tapped the baton on his music stand and stared out towards the newcomer. I turned back and waited.

"It seems we have a new member." Anthony, sixty now and gaunt, his face pinched and greyish in the thin light. He looked peeved rather than disturbed. I looked around me again and noticed the male choir members seemed as energised by the man's singing as the women appeared depleted. They stood, shoulders pushed back, chests puffed forward.

The stranger at the back said nothing.

"We can discuss the formal audition process in the break," Anthony said, "but I'm afraid we're mid-rehearsal at present." He peered out over his glasses. "You could come nearer so we can at least see you."

The man walked forward to the edge of the nave lanterns' reach. He had a high forehead that jutted above his eyes, shading them, and longish hair swept back. "I can audition as you sing. I know the piece well. If I'm not good enough, you can tell me afterwards."

Of course he'd be good enough; Anthony would be mad not to snap him up. His voice was extraordinary, for all there was something unsettling about it, and tenors are rare beasts nowadays. That night, we were down by three. The storm had worried them, localised flooding, one had apologised to me when he'd phoned. "You know how it is," he'd said, "with a small runabout car on these roads."

This new man appeared to be a Godsend, although even then I was uneasy about the nature of the God who might have sent him. We needed him, for sure, but why had he come to us? There were bigger, better choirs within travelling distance. Even from the little we'd heard, I knew he would be a superb soloist. What did we have that he might want?

Anthony was still looking nettled and I felt a sudden compulsion to intervene in case ruffled pride got the better of him, and he turned the stranger away. It was never wise to contradict Anthony, but even as I tried to suppress the urge, I found I was clearing my throat ready to break the silence.

"Couldn't we bend the rules, Anthony, and skip the formal audition just this once? We are short on tenors and there's no doubt he can sing."

Stella gave me a smile of encouragement and squeezed my arm. The rest of the choir looked as if they were waiting for my annihilation. I stared Anthony out. As Chorale secretary, I was used to handling his tirades when people sent their excuses before rehearsals, or the printing of programmes went awry. And besides, he had a soft spot for me – if he'd not had that dowdy little wife, who knew what might have been?

Anthony glared at me but raised his baton. The choir members readied themselves and smoothed their scores open. Our organist played a few bars of the orchestral introduction to lead us into the choral part, and we began again.

My memories of that evening shift their pattern every time I return to them. It's as if they're in a kaleidoscope, and each turn changes the weighting of the elements, one against another. I remember the physical feel of the night: the stone-chill air leaching us of warmth; the slight frowsty smell of Stella's cardigan; our singing, the best I'd ever heard us; the complex harmonies of the organ. And above all of it, all other sensations, the sound of the man's superhuman voice: powerful enough to swell the tenor line to full strength but still so soft that it felt like fingertips stroking over skin.

There was no possession this time, no mental connection, and I felt a little foolish, thinking that I'd imagined it, or at least exaggerated it. I knew I was susceptible to finding emotional release in music; I must have dropped my guard.

At the break, the man stepped out of his obscurity at the

back, and came forward into the weak, amber light from the side lamps. His hair, I could see now, was thick and dark, apart from four distinct pale streaks where the pigment was missing: not through age, I thought, because he seemed too young for that: far younger than I was then, fast coming up to fifty. He was taller than anyone else in the choir and dwarfed Anthony when he stood beside him in the aisle. He told us his name was Kai, and I guessed Scandinavian although he had no accent. Anthony was comradely to him now, wanting to secure his prize. I could see the light of victory in Anthony's eyes, an avaricious look, as if he had chanced upon gold in a sieve full of dirt.

When Stella and I were driving home, I asked her the question that had been bothering me all evening. Why had Kai chosen our choir? She considered as she drove down empty streets to the suburb at the edge of the small city where we both lived. Stella always drove. I liked a glass of wine with my supper before choir. It sharpened my attention and put energy into my voice. Stella didn't drink and said she was happy to drive. I bought her the occasional trinket as a thank-you.

"I think," Stella said, "he might be lonely. Perhaps he's new to the area – we might be a modest choir, but we're friendly and we'd always make a new member welcome."

"Anthony was hardly welcoming."

"He was a little put out at first, but Kai seemed to win him over." She paused at Kai's name, and her hands moved unnecessarily on the steering wheel.

Well, well. I watched her expression; she was hopeless at hiding anything. Well, well. It wasn't just me, then, he'd got to all of us. Even Stella.

2.

One man with a dream, at pleasure,
Shall go forth and conquer a crown.

By the time Kai found us, I had known Stella for around ten years. We'd met through choir and I doubt if we would ever have made friends without that chance inclination in both of us to sing for pleasure in the company of others. I had always been in one sort of choir or another – school, light operatic - but it was choral music I enjoyed most and so when I'd moved to a new research job in this city and heard about the Chorale, I'd been keen to join. Stella introduced herself to me, found that we lived near each other and suggested that we could travel together, and perhaps have a meal before rehearsal. I accepted, and Stella and I became an unlikely pair of friends.

Stella looked little changed that November than when I'd first met her: some wisps of grey in her dull brown hair, but few lines on the smooth roundness of her face. I'd secretly nicknamed her Dish Face when she first came to choir: she reminded me of an illustration in a nursery rhyme book I'd had when small: the dish who had run away with the spoon. A circular face with small, smiling features bunched in the centre.

Did I believe in evil, back then? I can't remember – I'd probably have thought of it as a twist in psychology; genes; freak wiring. I do know that when I met Stella, I came to believe in good. Watching her fascinated me: she seemed to have been born with a simple capacity for kindness, unselfishness, seeing the best in others; an uncorrupted soul.

Perhaps it was genetic. Stella's parents had been the same, awash with a compulsion to help the underdog. All three of them had spent most of their spare time in some kind of voluntary service: they'd helped at homeless shelters on Christmas Day, they'd visited the elderly, they'd taken the sick to hospital. No broken wing was safe from Stella's bindings, no soul went unsaved if there was half a chance Stella could drag it to salvation. Her purity was like one of nature's smooth, undisturbed surfaces – snow, perhaps, or sand – and for ten years I'd been fighting an impulse to stamp on it and spoil it.

There was never any hint of a boyfriend – or girlfriend – and until I watched her reaction to the mention of Kai, the tell-tale restlessness in her hands, her lip-parted gasp when she'd first heard him singing, I'd thought she was immune to any sort of physical attraction. It appeared that I was wrong.

Stella needed all her concentration to drive in the foul weather, and we travelled without speaking after our first exchange. The storm was dying, but it had left a legacy of standing water where leaf-clogged drains had failed to cope, or the sheer force of the deluge had overwhelmed escape routes. Twigs crunched like bones under the small car's wheels, branches lay dismembered across the pavements. The street lamps diffused a hazy spectral light that bled into the oily surface of pooled rainwater. Stella's silence irritated me. I wanted to discuss Kai, and whether he might be lonely.

"I suppose you're expert at the signs of loneliness," I said, "working where you do." Stella had a part-time role as receptionist in a counselling centre. A kind of triage, a first point of contact, perfect for her, with her serene smile and naively accepting nature. "Is that why you diagnosed him as needing company? Joining with us instead of a bigger, more impersonal outfit?"

"Perhaps." She paused to negotiate a roundabout. "Actually, I've seen him before. He has such a distinctive look with that white in his hair. He was outside the centre a couple of days ago - I wondered if he was a potential walk-in – we do get them sometimes if people feel desperate. I went out to speak to him when I'd finished my phone call, but he'd disappeared. I was glad to see him tonight, there was something about the intense way he'd been staring that had worried me."

I said I hadn't thought he looked at all distressed. That he'd seemed rather sure of himself, if anything.

"Well, I might be wrong," Stella said, "it might not be anything to do with his state of mind. He might have commitments which would stop him travelling to find a more high-profile choir. Work, or family."

"He wasn't wearing a wedding ring."

Anyone normal would have teased me for noticing. Stella said nothing. We reached my street and Stella pulled over to the wrong side of the road so that I wouldn't have to exit into a puddle. The pollarded lime trees splayed unnatural stunted limbs above us, a vague threat in their uneven, bunched fists.

"See you next week, then," I said. "I wonder if Kai will come back."

"Why wouldn't he?"

"Because we're second rate, because most of the members are pretty well geriatric -"

"They all do their best," Stella said, "and it's not as if we're professionals. He must have researched our standard before he came along."

"I suppose he must." I clicked open the car door and recoiled from the fierce rush of the wind. "I stand corrected, as ever." My irritation with her grew. She never seemed to resent my snippy comments - what would anyone have to do to get under that irreproachable skin?

I shut the door and held my hand up in farewell. The answer came to me as I crossed the road, head down against the gale, and remembered Stella's skittish, betraying hands moving on the steering wheel. Kai could do it. I reckoned that Kai could get inside Stella, body and soul, without doing anything much at all. And then the thought came to me as clearly as if someone had voiced it: And it would be so easy for me to help him.

3

For each age is a dream that is dying,
Or one that is coming to birth.

Week two of Kai started with supper at Stella's. We always
ate together before choir, alternating between her house and
my own. There was a great deal of beige chez Stella. Beige
laminate units, putty coloured floors, buff upholstered
sofas. It was like eating dinner in a vat full of porridge. If
Stella had a flaw, and God knows I'd tried hard enough to
find one, it was a complete lack of interest in anything friv-
olous, and that included interior décor and fashion. That
night she was wearing trousers that were so unflatteringly
awful I could hardly bear to look at her: perma-creased and
elastic-waisted, made of some man-made material the same
shade as unharvested barley gone off in the rain.

Having supper at Stella's was a mixed blessing for me. It
allowed me a night away from cooking, and I enjoyed the
sensation of being looked after, of treating myself to a glass
of wine with a dinner that someone served to me, but the
food tended towards the same colourless, flavourless inclination as its surroundings, and I found myself longing for a

punch of spice, or the bite of garlic. I brought my own wine with me, screw-capped, and I kept to the same brand, so that Stella, should she notice, would think I kept the same bottle week to week and took no nips of it in between. The truth was somewhat different, but I didn't want Stella to think I was anything like one of the hopeless drinkers who turned up at her centre every day.

I'd felt particularly spiteful and nasty all week and couldn't work out what might have caused it; it seemed to have a momentum of its own and I found myself wanting to have some sport with Stella, to force her to acknowledge that she had a fancy for Kai.

She served anaemic macaroni cheese with a side of white bread and butter, and I picked my moment three mouthfuls in, and after a slug of my Merlot.

"Are you looking forward to seeing Kai again?" I said. "I've heard from Anthony, Kai is definitely coming back. I must say, you seemed very taken with him last week."

"He has a lovely voice."

"He does - but don't you think it was more than that?" She looked at me, unusually wary. "Don't you think it was kind of thrilling? In a physical way, I mean?" She dropped her gaze, and I pressed my advantage, lying without a qualm. It was true Kai had had an effect on me, but labelling it as physical was too simplistic. How could I ever describe that feeling of connection with him, of being filled with no thoughts, or will, but his? The feeling that he had left a little of himself behind. "I don't mind admitting to you that I felt excited by the end of the evening. His voice has the knack of getting deep inside you. Do you know what I mean?"

I watched as a slow flush crept up from the collar of her blouse, mottled her neck, stained the round, flattish cheeks with erratic dots of crimson.

"Do you know what I mean?" I said again.

She took a forkful of macaroni, looked at it, rejected it and laid it back on her plate. "Yes."

"What are you going to do about it?"

Her mouth opened, a trace of butter gleamed on her lower lip. "What could I do?"

"I was wondering if you might make a bit of a play for him - you know."

"Play?"

I smiled at her and paused, choosing my words. I told her how this could be her time now, time for a little living and fun.

"Why not?" I said. "Your parents are gone and you've got no other ties."

"But I've never been the sort of woman that men like."

My smile widened; my voice was silky. She had so much in common with Kai, I told her. They both sang, they were both single, or so we believed Kai to be. "Maybe you've not met the right sort of man for you before," I said. "Show him you're interested - who knows what might happen?"

Her eyes widened. She had small, insipid eyes; if they could have been beige, they would have been, but nature had settled on a light uncertain grey. The flush over her face had matured into blotches.

"Really? You think a man like him might like me? In that way?"

I picked up my glass, and stalled answering by drinking. I felt at that moment that I was holding a stick; that I had two clear choices. I could lay down that stick, make an anodyne reply and change the subject, and that small discouragement would be enough to send Stella back to her normal world where men didn't want her, and she never expected them to, or I could poke the stick deep down in the undisturbed sediment at the heart of her and stir, stir, stir.

She was staring at me, willing me to answer. Willing me to make the answer she wanted to hear.

I felt a recklessness come over me then, a power that

someone's life and emotions were balanced on the edge of my fingertip and one tiny flutter of my hand would set off a chain of reactions. The sliver of ice inside me grew and I had a sense that Kai was near us, listening.

I said, "I'll invite him to supper before choir next week and we'll see what happens when he has a chance to get to know you."

"What about you?"

"What about me?"

"I thought you liked him too."

"Not particularly. He's all yours if you want him." Another lie. I hadn't completely sorted out my complicated feelings about Kai. I wasn't planning to compete, but I supposed there was nothing to stop me making a play for him as well, if the fancy took me that way.

"Well," Stella said at last, "if you think he might like to come, supper with him would be lovely. It's a kind thing for you to offer anyway, in case I was right first time and he is lonely."

Kind? I wasn't being kind on any level. I was striking a match and waiting to watch the paper burn.

I drank down the rest of my wine. Neither Stella nor I seemed to have appetite for the rest of the congealing supper. She cleared away, and we set off in the darkness to the cathedral.

And already goes forth the warning
That ye of the past must die.

It was on the second run through that it happened. Anthony was on fine form, lit up with the presence of Kai and his transformation of our sound, and his exhilaration transferred to his singers; we took deeper breaths, sang out from our stomachs to make our voices rich and even. We watched the baton, took our cues, were spot-on with our timing. Kai was out of my eyeline on the tenor back row; I had no way of seeing him as I sang, but at the end of the first section as we ran through from the top, an image of him appeared in my mind so vividly that I turned around to make sure he was still there, at the back, and had not moved to stand in front of me. He returned my gaze coolly, as if he had expected me to turn; I looked back towards Anthony and his baton, but the image remained.

There was something in Kai's expression, a kind of insolence, that put me on edge, and for some reason, made me turn my head to look at Stella. What I saw happen startled me so much I stopped singing, and simply stared. She was standing straight, with her face tip-tilted up towards the hidden height of the tower. Her eyes were open, but blank and unfocused, soulless, as if an essential part of her was missing; her arms spread slightly out from her sides, palms up, accepting. She was singing in perfect time and harmony with the choir, and word-perfect, despite the score lying abandoned on her chair. As I watched, her mouth widened into a smile of such lascivious delight that I, too, looked up, to see if something remarkable might be in her view. When I turned my head towards her again, she inclined towards me and met my gaze. The smile faded, her eyes hardened into a sly, malicious stare and as she sang out, her spittle struck my cheek like a spray of bile.

At the break, I went to find Anthony with some vague intention of telling him how peculiar Stella was being. He was standing alongside his lectern; his eyes shone, alive with energy, and he gazed over at Kai like a fanatic adulating his leader. He gushed praise, how marvellous Kai was, how he could be the making of the choir. Kai had told him that he knew others who might like to join us, accomplished singers like him.

"He doesn't strike me as a man with friends," I said.

"I don't see how you can tell that without knowing anything about him."

The experience of observing Stella's strange transformation had drained me so much I was having trouble standing up. I moved away from Anthony and slumped into one of the front pews.

Anthony regarded me. "Are you all right?"

"I don't know."

"If you're coming down with something you'd better get home. I don't want you spreading it to the rest of the choir and ruining the rehearsal schedule."

"You're all heart."

"I'm only thinking of the greater good. A choir is not a collection of individuals, it's an entity of its own, and I have to think of the health of that body, not yours, mine or anyone else's."

Another wave of exhaustion washed over me, and I stared up at him. Giving up and going home seemed a suddenly attractive prospect – perhaps Anthony was right, and I was sickening for something; perhaps I was so feverish I'd imagined the whole strange incident.

I said, partly to myself, "I don't think we should trust Kai."

"What on earth do you mean?"

"I don't know. I'm still trying to work out what I mean."

Anthony was impatient with me. What harm could Kai possibly do to us? Sabotage? Spying? His sarcasm piled on.

I was ridiculous; we were a choral society, not bloody MI5.

I closed my eyes. "It's difficult to explain, but he's after something, and he's using us – our singing – to get it."

"Stella likes him," Anthony said. "She's deep in conversation with him now."

The floor melted away from me as I remembered. The supper invitation! Stella would have lost no time in going over to him to follow up on our discussion, and I knew now, with complete certainty, that I did not want Kai in my house. I had a sudden feeling of being at war with myself. Kai attracted me, but he was starting to disturb me too. The power of him, the way he seemed to infiltrate my mind and incite me to acting in ways I might otherwise be able to suppress. Perhaps it was not too late to turn the tide; to protect myself, and in doing that, I could be a good friend and protect Stella.

I stood up, caught the side of the pew for support, and steadied myself. "I'll be okay. Stella's driving, so I'll have to stay until the end. I'm fine, really."

I walked to the shadows before the altar where Kai and Stella were standing. She was so much shorter than he was, and had her face turned up towards him. They stopped talking as I approached and watched me. Stella had a look of mild annoyance, and Kai was smiling a secretly amused kind of smile. It was plain that neither of them wanted me there.

Kai said, "Stella has invited me to supper at your house next week before our rehearsal." His eyes were pale grey, the colour of a sunless sky. There were no lines around them, no signs of ageing on his skin. His gaze was unfriendly, and held, I thought, a warning.

"I'm sorry, I forgot to say earlier," I said to Stella. "I'm having some work done in the kitchen so I won't be able to cook next week."

"That's not a problem, I can make supper at my house again." She turned to Kai. "I lost my parents last year so I'm a free agent now and the house is mine. I'd love to cook for you."

The adoration in her eyes was nauseating and I felt my stomach contract. He told her how delighted he was, how he would look forward to coming. I walked away, my thoughts churning.

Stella drove faster than normal on the way home. Usually, she was careful after dark, and considerate – over considerate, I'd always thought, as she stopped to let streams of traffic out from side roads or waited until elderly people had both feet on the opposite pavement before she proceeded over a crossing. Tonight, she accelerated past junctions, and went through pedestrian lights on amber. I wasn't sure whether she was merely distracted, or whether she had undergone some subtle change.

She made no attempt at conversation so after a few minutes I broke into the silence. "Did something odd happen to you tonight?"

"I don't think so."

"Are you sure?" I paused, seeking for a way of describing what I had witnessed without sounding like a complete lunatic. "Have you ever had something go wrong with your computer, and a technician has taken it over remotely to fix it? And you sit there, watching the cursor zoom about and click on things, and you're not doing anything to cause it? I was watching you tonight – after the break – and you looked just like that. Like someone had taken you over."

"What a very strange thing to say."

"You were even singing without your music, like it was automatic."

"So I've memorised my part -"

"I think it was something to do with Kai. I can't say why, but I do. Call it an instinct for danger."

She said that she'd felt nothing unusual that evening,

nothing at all. Anthony had mentioned I was coming down with something. She thought he might be right seeing as I seemed to be delusional. She could see I was pale under my make-up, my lips looked bloodless. Was I feeling sick? I told her that Anthony was talking nonsense, that I was fine in body, but my mind was troubled.

"I watched you!" I said. "You looked so strange, and I think that somehow, Kai caused it. Are you really telling me the truth? You felt nothing?"

"I felt nothing unpleasant tonight," she said carefully, "although I did feel unusually connected with our singing. As Kai has made such a difference to our sound already, perhaps it was to do with him, but it was an uplifting, fulfilling experience. You're making it out to be something – demoniacal."

"That's what it looked like - a sort of temporary possession."

Her face was half-hidden in the dim car interior, but I could see she was smiling. The same sly way she had smiled earlier. The same smile as Kai's.

I said, "What's so amusing?"

"I think you're jealous."

"Jealous?"

"Yes, jealous. Because Kai's taken a liking to me and not

you."

I stared at her. Was this really Stella? "Good heavens, what's got into you? This isn't like you!"

"How do you know what's like me? When have you ever taken the trouble to find out what I'm really like? All you do is sneer at me. You look at me sometimes as if I'm one of your lab specimens!"

"That's not true!" I said, although part of it hit home. "I've always respected your kindness, the way you care for others, your – goodness. Your good soul."

She rounded on me. As we passed by intermittent streetlights, I saw lines of anger deepen alongside her mouth. Her hands gripped the steering wheel, her knuckles were sharp under her skin. She was sick of being good, she said. Sick of being unselfish, sick of always thinking of others. Like I'd said, it was time for her to live a little. As she'd said, I was jealous because Kai hadn't singled me out. I was trying to put her off.

I was, that last bit was true enough. But, I told her, it was only for her own good.

"My own good? How dare you!"

I said nothing. Stella in this mood – in this guise – was an unknown quantity and I needed to reflect on how best to approach her. Not with confrontation or honesty, evidently.

She pulled up outside my house so close to the lime tree on the pavement that I had to insinuate myself from the car like a wraith. I was in too much turmoil to bid her goodbye, but she opened her own door, stepped out, and looked at me over the roof of the car.

"I'd rather you didn't come next week, to supper. I'd rather it was just Kai."

"And I suppose you'd rather I drove myself to choir?"

"I would."

I was at a loss now, shaking and suddenly weak. I wanted to shout, childlike, "Can't we make friends again?" but I couldn't trust myself to speak. Stella climbed back into the car, slammed the door, and drove away.

I stood in the road and watched the tail lights of her hatchback diminish, and it seemed to be a metaphor for the ten years of our friendship fading out of sight.

My house was a thirties semi in a long avenue of similar semis: not identical, as people had made them individual over the years, but still part of a whole. Only mine was unlit. The others, some with curtains open, some closed, glowed warm and welcoming in the damp November air. Family homes, with people inside who cared for each other.

I thought of Stella driving away, her head full of feelings for Kai, and dislike of me, and the thought of what my spark of vindictiveness, teasing her to make a play for Kai, had led to, was like a kick to my stomach. I shook my head. Feeling like this was making me uncomfortable and anyway, it was pointless if I really thought about it. What was I really losing? A half-baked connection between two unequal partners? She'd never been a person I'd liked to be seen about with. In truth, I'd always been rather ashamed of my friendship with her. And we'd had so little in common. Kai was welcome to her.

The immediacy of Kai's presence and singing was fading and any idea that there was something supernatural about him was beginning to look foolish. He was a man, nothing more, and if I could find out who he was, I could bring him back to earth.

For we are afar with the dawning
And the suns that are not yet high

The next day, at work, I started searching on the web. I only had Kai's first name, and so I phoned Anthony on a flimsy excuse about Chorale subscriptions and asked if he knew Kai's name in full. He hesitated, searched his memory for a few moments and then had to admit, he didn't. Whether

Kai had told him, and he'd forgotten, or whether he had neglected to ask in the excitement and unconventionality of Kai's arrival, he couldn't recall, but the net result was that the man was just Kai, and that was it.

I did my best. Kai is an unusual name, but not unknown, and although my search threw up a few suspects, none of them were obviously the man who'd turned up in the cathedral. I dived into social media profiles, dissected obscure news reports, but there was nothing. As far as I could see the man had no past and no present. No life, before and outside his relationship with our choir.

My next searches were around the powers of choral singing and telepathic transference. Choir membership did seem to have magical properties: it could help mental health problems, act as a cathartic mechanism for trauma. Nowhere was there a mention of music being used as a forced entry to the mind or soul, and my telepathy research was inconclusive, really someone's wishful belief dressed up as science.

I ended up feeling defeated and dissatisfied and left work early, pleading a headache. I'd slept barely a few minutes the night before, my mind was spinning with doubt and confusion, I'd developed a tremor in my hands and my body felt chill to the bone, despite the full-on radiator in my office. Whatever I said about Kai, it was unlikely that anyone would believe me, especially as I didn't really believe myself. Perhaps there was little I could do but watch him with Stella and see if I could guess his purpose.

4

They had no divine foreshadowing
Of the land to which they are going:

The following week, Stella and Kai were late for choir. So late, that Anthony had delayed the start of the rehearsal and was stamping about demanding "Where is he?" to the choir members in general, and to me in particular.

I shrugged. I had no idea. I'd tried to contact Stella several times a day during the week, but she'd left her phone unanswered and not responded to any texts or mails. I'd driven to the counselling centre, but I'd not managed to catch sight of her entering or leaving, and it was impossible to see inside. Privacy was key in that place: vertical blinds, obscured glass. Part of me wouldn't have been surprised if Stella had vanished, swallowed up into Kai's head, and never came to choir again.

When they did arrive, Anthony stopped pacing and greeted them as if it were he who'd been the bad timekeeper and had wanted to start the rehearsal too early. Stella was flushed: from the nip in the wind outside, from the ostentatious entrance and half-run up the aisle towards us, perhaps from some other activity it was better not to imagine. A colour heightened by stirred emotion would have suited most pallid women, but not Stella. She'd tried to use make-up, and it looked like an adolescent's first attempt: lips which were lined outside their contours into a haphazard Cupid's bow, eyebrows like circumflexes. I wondered whether she'd also had a go at contouring with blusher and highlighter, but realised that, actually, her face was thinner. Still flat, but less round, as if she'd had the edges shaved into harsh straight lines. What was it – was she on a crash diet to lose her dumpiness for Kai? Kai, arriving just behind her, held a challenge in his eyes when he regarded me. Look, it seemed to say, look what I've caught.

Stella was apologising to Anthony and fishing out her score from her bag. She told him how sorry she was for their lateness, but how proud she thought he'd be of them. They had been practising at her house, three times that week. Kai, she said, had gone over the phrasing with her. She felt Anthony would be pleased at the improvement. Perhaps she could lead the sopranos instead of me?

"You've been singing together?" I said, and my voice came too loud and blunt. "You've been alone with Kai's voice?"

"What an odd way to put it," Stella said, and I was aware of the choir members' interest, as if they'd started following a game and were struggling to make out the rules, "but, yes. And he has been alone with mine. Shall we start?"

Our sound that night was outstanding. Two of the tenors who'd been missing the week before had returned – bolstered, I suspected, by the news that they'd acquired a brilliant new colleague who'd deflect Anthony's attention, and stop him from focusing on their duff notes and inconsistent breathing. Stella's practice with Kai had paid off: her voice was sure, effortless on the top notes, rich on the lower. By the break, it was apparent that only I was struggling: it was as if some essential component part of me had been stolen. I looked at Stella who was being fussed over by two of our fellow sopranos. Whatever I'd lost, she seemed to have gained. I couldn't see Kai. He had a knack of fading into the shadows when it suited him, and it had struck me the week before that he evaded contact with the others as much as he could. Apart from Stella. And, in a different way, me.

Anthony waved his hand at me. A summons. I went over to him. Close to, I could see he wasn't smiling.

"You're singing flat."

I took a step back. "I'm what?"

"Singing flat. I can hear you a semitone below the rest of them. Good job Stella's raised her game so much this week otherwise you'd be leading all the sopranos off-key."

"I never sing flat."

I was not one of the normal offenders, he agreed, but I was tonight. He wanted a better effort in the second half or he'd be shaming me publicly.

My throat constricted; my eyes burned. The thought of crying in front of them all horrified me. The only immediate antidote was anger.

"You're only getting at me because I'm not fawning over Kai like the rest of you. I tell you, that man is dangerous."

He frowned at that. His reply held a threat: I should be careful. I should remember how I could be erratic sometimes – how I'd been caught out in the past.

He said, "I can't risk you alienating Kai – or Stella, for that matter. Her voice is wonderful when she relaxes and feels confident. You don't have to like the man or enjoy the fact he seems to be favouring Stella over you, but if you want to stay in for *The Music Makers*, you're going to have to put yourself and your likes and dislikes second, and the choir first."

I nodded, turned, and walked back to my place in the soprano section. There was nothing I could have said in response even if I'd found the strength to say it.

I stood in the front row of the sopranos, Kai was, as

usual, in the back line of the tenors. I tried to concentrate on my score, on keeping my notes exactly true, but every now and again, I felt a compulsion to look back towards Kai: the same kind of compulsion I might have felt if I'd known that there was an unpredictable animal behind me. A snake, or a wolf waiting to spring. Each time I glanced away from my music, Kai was staring at me. Eventually, I willed myself not to look at him for the remainder of the rehearsal, kept my shoulders back, sang from as deep in my body as I could manage and stayed more or less in tune until the end.

The question that preoccupied me for the next couple of days was, why? Why was Kai so keen to get Stella alone? She was no beauty and had so little real personality, what did she have to offer a man like him? It wasn't until Saturday afternoon, and I bought a weekend paper, that I had what I thought was a revelation.

The headline read: Con man defrauds widow of life savings. I spread out the paper on my kitchen table and took in the story. A fraudster had persuaded a widow to fall for him, enticed her to invest in a bogus business venture and had then disappeared with the spoils. She was, she told the reporter, not just desolate and alone, but destitute. I stopped reading and stared away from the paper, out of the window, watching absently as the conifers in my narrow scrubby garden bowed in the wind.

Stella. Stella was rich. When her parents had died, they had left her their solid Victorian villa, but there had been a great deal more to Stella's parents than had been obvious to a casual visitor to their house. Her father had been an inventor, had hundreds of patents to his name, and some had made him remarkably well off. Modest in their ways, it appeared that they'd never grasped exactly how wealthy they were, which was fortunate, it seemed to me, as given their charitable tendencies, they'd probably have given most of it away. Now, it had come to Stella and unlikely though it seemed to look at her, she was extraordinarily wealthy. And Kai, I realised now, was likely to be the most prosaic and clichéd of predators: somehow, he'd found out about her, and he was after her money. It explained why she'd seen him hanging around outside the counselling centre. He must have targeted her from the first and worked out that joining the Chorale was a good way of getting to her. What a piece of luck for him that he was such a gifted singer.

I sat back in my chair. My skin was clammy and once again, I felt that chill that had been plaguing me since Kai had seemingly invaded my mind at choir. I was still sleeping badly. Every creak in the night made me start; I fancied I could hear windows blow open in the wind, or the front door lock unfasten, but when I crept down to check, there was nothing. I went no further: there was a limit to my bravery. I couldn't bring myself to activate the outdoor light with its angled beam trained on the garden; I couldn't face the thought of what – or who – I might see hiding there.

As usual, I had no particular plans for the evening, so I bought a take-away tuna salad from the supermarket and made my way to Stella's house.

There are some streets where sitting and watching is easy, and Stella's was one of the best. On estates, for example, like the one where Anthony lives, the road is too exposed. The front garden walls are low, there are no laurel hedges or privet screens. Anthony's has a front lawn that slopes down to join the pavement and his neighbours' houses in the cul de sac are the same. The neighbourhood watch is active; every unrecognised parked car is remarked on, as mine had been. He'd tackled me about it after choir, and I'd had no explanation he'd have understood, although it was simple, really: it was the looking on that attracted me, the feeling that I was a small hidden part of another's life. It gave me a little excited lift every time I thought about what I'd seen, and knew, and that they'd had no idea I was out there. Harmless, for all that some people seemed to find it disturbing.

As I'd expected, Stella's house presented no problems. I stopped the car on the opposite side of the road and had a fine view both ways. There were no lights on upstairs or in the sitting room, the hallway was lit, and the outside lamp switched on. That was a giveaway. Stella had inherited more than money from her parents: she'd inherited thrift, too, and no light was ever on unnecessarily. She was expecting company, and that company was certainly not me. I opened my plastic tub of dinner and waited.

I must have been distracted for a moment; I'd seen no sign of Kai walking up the street but as I looked up from chasing the last forkful of vinegary salad around its bowl, he was there, by the front door. Stella's lamp had him in a spotlight; the strong beam picked out the white streaks in his hair, freakish against the darkness of the rest of his head and body. He was wearing a loose overcoat that flowed out from his shoulders and appeared in silhouette like a gown, or a cape. Odd, and old-fashioned.

Stella opened the door wide, over-dramatically, as if she were throwing apart stage curtains ready to perform. I raised my binoculars and had a clear view of the long hallway, two-tone, beige above the dado, sludge brown below. Stella's face was radiant. She had changed her hairstyle, had had a fringe cut in across the smooth flat forehead and had curled the rest of her hair. Even at a distance, I could see she was wearing garish red lipstick, and she was definitely thinner; it suited her. Kai greeted her with a brief kiss on the cheek and entered. The door shut on the pair of them and I felt it like a slap.

It was cold in the car, but I didn't want to risk the engine. I kept a wool throw on the back seat, and wrapped it across me, willing them to come into the front sitting room, willing Stella not to close the curtains.

My wish was partially granted when the light in the sitting room flicked on and Stella walked over to the window. She stared out for a moment, and although I knew that the brightness behind her would blind her to the road outside, that she could not possibly see me across the street, and that, in any case, she was unfamiliar with my car as she'd always been the driver when we'd travelled to choir, despite all my certainty in my invisibility, I shrank back into my seat and dared not raise my binoculars again. Kai came in and stood behind her, looming over her short, thick figure. I kept still, virtually not breathing, until Stella reached up and pulled the curtains across as theatrically as she had opened the door earlier. Whatever she and Kai were intending to do, they would be doing it in private. Almost. She had been slapdash with her curtain-closing: there was a triangle of light still showing at the bottom where the curtains met the sill. Enough to see through, if I was careful. Enough to find out exactly how far this affair, if that's what it was, had gone.

I left the car and opened the gate, pulling and releasing the catch slowly to stifle its click. Adjoining the path were a few feet of wintery grass; I tacked sideways, up to the window, and knelt down in the empty, damp earth below the bay. My triangular view was enough to see the central part of the room, to see a bottle of wine and glasses on a table, to see Stella and Kai standing close-up together, their arms touching as they held music scores in front of them. Kai sang a few notes to lead Stella in and I watched her face as they began to sing together.

There was joy in her expression at first, pure elemental joy, but as I watched, that joy seemed to darken, become something contorted: rotten and perverted, as if the core of her was changing into something I could hardly dare acknowledge. Their music quickened. They were singing parts from a chorus I didn't recognise – something strong and compelling, with a striking harmony at the end of the phrasing. There was a union of them as they sang, beyond the physical: they still stood side by side, fully dressed, with no attempt at intimate contact, but it was as if they'd gone beyond any need for sexual satisfaction. They had everything they needed in the sound that the two of them were making. For the moment, the two, it seemed to me, had fused into one.

> *That we dwell in our dreaming and singing*
> *A little apart from ye.*

Their music-making was for them alone. Kneeling on the wet ground in the chill winter air, I was excluded from all of it, their togetherness, the strange ecstasy of the singing. I crawled to the path and pulled myself up. My breathing was rough, my pulse rapid and I had to force myself back to the car, to climb in and turn the engine on to warm me. After a few moments, I locked the doors and found strength enough to drive away.

My house was unlit, as usual, a sad lonely island of darkness. I rushed in, turned on all the lights, cranked the heating up to tropical. Both my televisions blared out a quiz programme – I couldn't cope with the thought of anything that might involve music. I boiled the kettle without any clear intention of what to do with it. I ran a bath. Perhaps

I had crouched too long in that dank space below the mossy stone of Stella's bay window, perhaps the odd lewd hunger in Stella's face had chilled me quite literally, but my body had gone into convulsive shivering and I couldn't get warm. I lay in the bath, let the foam rise around my head and dampen my hair, and tried to block out the vision of them, remove the sound of their singing from my brain.

It took me an hour to come back to life. I topped up the water twice to keep it hot, half-listened to a debate on the radio, and finally pulled myself out. I felt raw, despite the heat in the bathroom. The air on my body shocked me, as if I were new-born and out of my natural element, unprotected. It was a disconcerting, rootless feeling, and the thought flashed through me that perhaps part of me had always been yearning for the safety of the womb, even for a nest lined with reluctance as my mother's had been. Longing for inclusion, however I might deny it and pretend to myself that I liked existing on my own. Melancholy washed over me. My body was cooling again; I scoured myself dry with a towel, and wandered back downstairs in a warmed cotton robe, thinking that a drink might buck me up.

Kai was in my kitchen.

I stopped in the doorway, realising that I had known

all along that this might happen; why I had been so alert recently for signs of intrusion, why, on my return, I'd filled the house with light, and heat, and noise, to leave no room for him and his manipulative presence. And it had failed.

He was leaning against my worktop, wearing the dark, cloak-like coat I'd seen him in earlier. Despite the heat, and the thickness of his clothing, he showed no sign of discomfort.

"You were at Stella's earlier. You were spying on us."

"You've no right to be in my house. I want you to leave. Now."

He shook his head. "Not yet. Why were you spying on us?"

"I asked you to leave."

"I'll leave – when I've heard your answer."

I felt the muscles in my legs weaken. My heart rate was furious, my mouth dry. I made a pantomime of walking casually to the kitchen table and pulling out a chair. I reckoned I was no more vulnerable sitting down, and at least it steadied me.

He was watching me with that small, amused smile that made my temper flare, despite my fear. It was remarkable how he could convey a physical threat even as he stood so still. How his eyes could mesmerise, his voice penetrate.

I told him that I'd rumbled him, and was worried for Stella, that he was out to cheat her of her inheritance. That he was a charlatan. A fraud. That's why I'd been watching.

"I'm out to defraud her? That's what you think?"

"Yes, of course I do. What else could you want from her apart from her money? I can't believe you're interested in her for any other reason."

"Because you don't think she is physically attractive?"

"Yes, if you like."

"As it happens, I've no interest in her money or her body."

He pushed himself away from the cupboard and I flinched. "Don't you dare come any nearer."

He stared at me for a too-long moment and I sensed that he was trying to win me over again, to turn me from antagonist into ally. I'd helped him once, without intending to. This time, I needed to keep myself apart. Please, God, don't let him start to sing.

I said, "If you are really not trying to exploit her for money or for sex, what do you want from her?"

"If you had any imagination, you could work it out."

"But those are the only two things any man ever wants from a woman."

"Not quite." He smiled; my pulse raced. "Let's just say

53

I want Stella because she is special. People as naturally good as Stella are rare in this world." He pulled the back door open – a thin shaft of iced air slid in; my skin shrank beneath my robe. "You should stop interfering now and leave us alone. You're too late, anyway, it's already gone too far."

The door shut, and he was gone. My strength left my body and I lay my head on the table. He'd beaten me, not physically, not even with the threat in his words, but with something else far more fundamental. My lack of understanding, of not being able to work out what a man could possibly want of a woman that was not money, and that was not sex."Is it love?" I shouted pointlessly at the door, its square panes blank in the darkness. "Is that what you meant? Do you love her? Is that what you want from her?" But he had gone, faded into the depths of the night, and I had no answer.

5

You shall teach us your song's new numbers,
And things that we dreamed not before.

I was late for the next choir rehearsal. I'd dithered over
going, so distracted that I'd misplaced my keys and took
a while to find them. It was week three of After Kai, and
although most of me was a confused mix of loss and resent-
ment, I had to admit that a small part remained objectively
curious. It was as if Kai was a catalyst in one of my experiments, and I was watching on, observing the reaction as he
met the pure substance that was Stella.

The rehearsal had started by the time I arrived but,
unlike Kai, I had no ability to enter the cathedral invisibly.
It was a still, subdued evening, the air so wet it was almost
as if a mist were hanging between the half-timbered walls in
the old alleyways around the cathedral. The west door was
pulled firm against the cold and I made my entrance at the
end of the first part of the rehearsal. The hollowed stone
bounced the sound of the door closing after me across the
nave; Anthony turned, all the choir members looked over
their scores at me. I walked the length of the aisle feeling as

if I were climbing the steps to the guillotine. Stella's expression held no welcome; Kai, at the back, seemed amused. I had to press past Stella to reach my place at the end of the row, and she recoiled as if I were contaminated. No one seemed able to look me in the eye.

At the break, I started over to Anthony to apologise for my late arrival, but he was already making his way to me. We met beyond the choir stalls, and he indicated to the left.

"I need to have a conversation with you. It'll be more private in the side chapel."

I followed him past the stone columns and into the smaller space. A carved wooden triptych shone gently in the half-light. The chapel was unheated, and I shivered.

Anthony noticed and said, "This won't take long. I'm afraid there's been a complaint made against you."

I stared at him, guessing what was coming next.

"By Stella," Anthony said. "She says you have been stalking her."

"That's not the case at all!"

"She says you were crouching outside her front window and spying on her – and Kai – as they practised."

I took a deep breath. "I was, but only once. That's hardly stalking. I'm trying to find out what's going on, what Kai's game is with her."

"And what was he doing to her when you invaded their privacy?"

"Singing. They were singing together."

"And she wasn't – being forced to sing against her will?"

I railed at his sarcasm. "No, but it's how he does it, how he influences her. He gets her to sing with him and then somehow joins up with her mind. I've seen it happen."

Anthony was staring at me. "Have you any idea how insane you're sounding?"

"I can see that it's difficult to understand unless you've witnessed it yourself, but trust me, he does."

"But what do you think he wants? None of this makes any sense whatsoever."

"I don't know. I haven't worked that out yet."

Anthony sighed. "Look, I know it must be disappointing for you if you'd developed a liking for him and he prefers Stella, but that's just how it is sometimes. You have to park it and move on."

"I'm not jealous! I'm trying to get you to see that you have to do something - it won't end well for Stella if you allow Kai to sing with her on their own."

Anthony took a step away from me. His face in the meagre chapel light was drained of all colour. He had a tic in one eye when he was nervous, and his eyelid pulsed now. "Allow? What do you think I could do about it, even if I wanted to? I'm a choirmaster, not a gaoler or a moral guardian." He indicated to a chair. "Will you sit down for a moment?"

"I'll stand, thanks."

"This is mad talk, you know. Accusations that Kai is taking over Stella's mind for some unknown purpose of his own, you spying on them - mad, dangerous talk." I opened my mouth to retort, but he stalled me with a hand. "And we have to acknowledge that it's happened before. The stalking part, anyway."

I shook my head. "That was different I – I just like watching sometimes, you know that. I never meant any harm that time -"

"It's not normal behaviour, for heaven's sake! Can't you see that? It caused huge problems for me when my wife caught you staking out our house, as you well know. I should probably never have let you stay in the Chorale, let alone remain as secretary, but I felt sorry for you."

I said nothing. I was well aware he'd always secretly desired me, but if that's how he wanted to represent it, there was nothing to say.

"I need to take Stella's complaint seriously. I was intending to anyway, but I don't like what I've been hearing about mind games. It's not rational."

I swallowed and asked him what he wanted me to do.

"I have to ask you to stay away from the Chorale - at least until after *The Music Makers*, and until you've sought some help. I really think you should do that."

"You'll lose Stella, you know. We all will. And Kai, when he's got what he came for."

He shook his head, sighed again, and said a few words about dignity, and irrationality, and delusion.

I turned my back on him then, fetched my bag and coat from my place, and left without talking to anyone. I'm sure they were all staring at me, but I didn't look back. I drove home, checked all the window locks and wedged chairs against the external doors although I knew by then it was a waste of time – no door or wall would prove an impediment to Kai.

6.

Till our dream shall become their present,
And their work in the world be done.

I took a week off work, and thought I'd try one more attempt to talk to Stella. Tracking her down proved difficult: I tried waiting for her outside the house on one of her working mornings, but she made no appearance. I went to the counselling service – they told me she'd resigned the week before, leaving immediately and giving no notice. I finally caught up with her on the night of choir rehearsal, running up the road and grabbing at her arm as she unlocked her car.

"Stella! Wait!"

She swore at me and pushed me away. She was stronger than I would have credited, her face was ugly with rage. I staggered back and only just managed to right myself without falling. I tried again, lunging out to clutch at her coat, but I was too unsteady to get much of a grip and stood, breathing painfully, as she wrenched the door shut and over-revved the engine to pull out into the traffic.

I closed my eyes. I'd lost her. Kai had won, Stella had chosen her path – wherever that might lead – and I had no idea whether I'd ever see either of them again.

7

Yea, in spite of a dreamer who slumbers,
And a singer who sings no more.

Almost two years passed after that last meeting. Winter once more, an icy snap at the end of November; bare trees and sparse, sharp air. It was a Friday evening and I was starting my slow preparations for bed. My life functions better within a system of routine: a meal at seven, TV at eight, turn the electric blanket on at nine ready for bed an hour or so later. My programme had finished, and I was pouring myself a whisky nightcap when the doorbell sounded. One long insistent ring, and then another. My muscles froze, and I stared down the hallway. Ten o'clock, not a time for innocent callers. I ran upstairs and pulled the bedroom curtains aside to see who might be standing under the security light. Stella.

I barely recognised her. She'd bleached her hair and it showed harsh and ashy under the strong light. She was heavily made-up and was dressed in a skimpy blouse and skirt. I hesitated, but curiosity, and perhaps some other buried emotion, gained the better of me. I descended the stairs, disengaged the safety chain, and opened the door.

She thrust past me and slammed the door behind her. She had no bag, or coat, and I saw a smear of blood along one pale arm and down the front of her blouse. The pupils of her eyes were dilated, and her gaze flicked around the hallway, nervous, unfocused. I could smell drink on her breath. She was breathing fast, inhaling on a catching sob, exhaling in a gasp. I opened my mouth to speak, but she cut me off.

"You've got to help me – I think I've just killed someone."

I stared at her.

"I ran them down as they were crossing the road – up there." She gesticulated north, towards the main road. "I could see them in the distance, but I thought they'd hurry up and get a move on – thought if I gunned for them they'd shift, but they didn't - and then it was too late. I hit them straight on …got out and saw there was blood everywhere and ran off, down here."

"What about your car?"

"I just left it – and my bag and everything."

"You'll have to go back! It's an offence to leave like that!"

"I can't."

"It's a natural reaction to run away, you're in shock. The police'll understand if you go back now."

"They won't. I lost my licence. Last year. I'd been drinking."

"And you've been drinking now - and by the look of your eyes, that's not all."

She said nothing. Her breathing was slowing, she slumped backwards against the wall.

I said, "What do you want me to do?"

"Can you let me stay here for tonight? Sleep it off, sort my head out so I can work something out."

I told her that there were things we could do, needed to do, such as call an ambulance for the victim who might still be alive, she should go back, hand herself in.

"I can't, I told you – no licence, drinking, it'll be prison again. I've already done that, can't do it again."

"Jesus, Stella, what's been happening to you?"

She shook her head. "Don't ask – just let me stay here, keep out of sight."

We stood in the hallway, both unmoving, gazes locked, until Stella looked away, then closed her eyes. I don't know how long we were standing there – it could have been seconds, or minutes. I heard Stella's breathing, the hall clock ticking – and then a distant sound, growing louder. A siren. Police or ambulance. Louder, then abruptly cut off.

"They've found him," I said. "Too late to go back now."

Her eyes were still closed. "It was a woman. She had fluffy white hair just like my mother's." Her face creased.

"Jesus fucking Christ."

The obscenity was so unexpected I think it startled me more than anything else had. "Stella," I said quietly, "You were such a good soul, you know. Back then."

She opened her eyes. The whites were bloodshot, pinkish and blurred under tears. "It was Kai. Each time we met up and sang together, he'd take something from me. Each time, afterwards, it was as if I'd got darker inside. I wanted to – do things – that I'd barely heard of before. It was like he got into my mind and was feeding off me, like he looked so – full, so satisfied – after we'd been together. Like he'd stolen something and used it to fatten himself up."

"You think Kai stole your goodness away?"

"Sounds far-fetched when you put it like that, but yes. I do. He hunts for souls, for good people. I think he collects them. He's like a vampire, but he needs pure souls to keep him going, not blood. You guessed he was dangerous. You tried to warn me."

I tried to keep my expression neutral. "Do you still see him?"

"Off and on. He turns up. He's not there, and then he is, I can never work out how he gets in or finds out where I am. I'm so frightened of seeing him again – I think that'll be it if it happens another time. He'll take the last tiny bit of the old me that's left."

I took in a breath, breathed out slowly. My thoughts were clearing, arranging themselves in order. I suggested a cup of tea for both of us, to buy us time while I thought of a plan. I turned off the hall light and shut us in the kitchen. Filled the kettle, clicked it on. Told her to sit down. Stella was obedient, as if she were operating on purely motor function. I worked in silence, and Stella made no attempt to speak.

Eventually, after I'd put a mug of tea and a couple of biscuits in front of her, I said, "I know what we'll do. You can stay here tonight. There's no reason for the police to trace you to my house immediately, if at all, and if we stay in here and keep the front lights off, it'll look as if there's no one in. Tomorrow, we can get you away if that's what you really want. It's easy enough to stay hidden if you have resources."

"I don't have any. I spent it all - Mum and Dad's money - all gone."

"Did Kai get you to spend money on him?"

"Money? No." She was vague, becoming dreamy. "That's one thing he wasn't after."

"I thought he was, at first. I thought that was his plan." She shook her head. "How am I going to get away without money?

I reassured her. I would sort that. She'd been my only friend for years, after all. I'd missed her, I hadn't liked being alone.

She rubbed her hand over her forehead. "You're being so kind. I never thought of you as kind. Good job you weren't like I was, Kai would have had you too. Do you believe me? About Kai? About him stealing innocent souls?"

I smiled at her. "No. I believe that you believe it, but I think there's a more rational explanation. My guess is that you'd been repressing stuff for years, being such a good girl all the time your parents were alive, and then he came along, and you just – lost it. Went off the rails."

"Really?" She sat up straighter.

"Really."

"You think I've invented the whole thing?"

I looked away. The sight of her hopeful, ruined face was almost unbearable. "You didn't invent Kai, but the rest, what's happened to you? Kai being some sort of devil? Perhaps blaming him was just your conscious mind trying to find a reason – an excuse, if you like – for everything you've done."

She was quiet for a moment then said, "So if I've been losing my sanity rather than my soul, there's a chance I can get better? Go back to how I was?" She put her hand on mine; it felt warm, trusting. "Will you help me to come back?"

There's no turning back time, I told her, but there could be a future. I talked about moving on, making amends. "I could help you now, could help you get away tomorrow like I said, but there is an alternative. I think you should consider handing yourself in. It's true you'll get another prison sentence, but when you're out, you can start again. You could stay with me here afterwards, let me help you. Your choice. Think about it tonight."

She said quietly, "And if I did imagine it all, I know I can stand up to Kai if I see him again and not be scared he's going to finish the job. God, I can almost believe it's all over. Thank you, thank you so much."

I stood up. "Drink your tea. I'll be back in a minute." And even as I left her, I realised that I still had a choice too. I still had a chance of redemption if I had the courage to take it.

I knew he'd be there, in the darkness of the hallway. I sensed him before my eyes adjusted, and then, I could see him standing by the stairs, facing me. My impulse to rebel faded as swiftly as it had arisen, lost in the force of his presence.

He smiled at me, and I returned it – almost as an equal. We had come a long way in two years.

"You look well," I said, "sleek, one might say. Successful." I remembered what he'd said back then, when he'd left my house: I want Stella because she is special. People as naturally good as Stella are rare in this world. I said, "She was a good catch."

"And so were you. In a different way."

"I nearly turned away, just then."

"I know. But I knew you'd turn back."

I thought how I was glad he'd come to find me after Stella had begun her fall from grace. I was ready to connect with him then, was so tired of existing on my own, fighting battles with my own nature. Before he'd sought me out on that moonless spring night I'd almost come to believe he'd been a figment of my imagination, but then, there he was, sitting in my unlit kitchen a few weeks after he and Stella had left the Chorale, and Anthony had let me re-join, and I'd given up my resistance.

"Do you understand what I needed now?" he'd asked.

"I think so," I'd said, "I've done a lot of thinking. I think we're similar, you and I, both predators – or perhaps scavengers. Vampires, in our own way. Feeding off any little bit of goodness that we might find. The only difference between us then was that you knew what you were doing, and I still had a lot to learn. I was always attracted to Stella's purity, but I didn't know why, or how to use it."

"You do now," he'd said, and that smile I'd felt so excluded from when I'd first met him, embraced me, and pulled me in, and the core of me hardened and darkened and grew cold to meet it. We were not quite equals, but my powers were growing.

I said, "There's a new member at choir. She fosters children – she's very sweet. I thought I might invite her for supper next week – and a run through of our part. We're doing *The Crucifixion*. Perhaps you'd like to join us?"

"Perfect." He inclined his head towards the kitchen. "Shall we go and find Stella now? It's time we ended it."

For reply, I began to sing, very low and gently, the final stanza of *The Music Makers*. Kai took up the tenor line, and I felt the familiar exhilaration as our consciousnesses joined. By the time I opened the kitchen door, our music was swelling, filling the hallway, the house, the world: those last two lines, especially for Stella.

We are the music makers
And we are the dreamers of dreams.

Acknowledgements

I would like to thank the following for taking time to read the early versions of *The Music Maker* and for offering such helpful feedback, suggestions and encouragement: Neil Kershaw; My Arvon friends, Sarah Baxter, Jane Cooper and Katherine Mezzacappa; Bridgnorth Writers' Group, especially Barbara Chapman; Deb Catesby; Sarah Lillywhite. I also would like to thank Writing West Midlands for their excellent Room 204 development programme, Matthew Pegg and Mantle Arts, Hazel Osmond for showing me that it can be done, Andrew Taylor for his encouragement and inspirational Gothic fiction and finally, my chief supporter, Meg Dunmore, and my family: Neil, Sarah, Hannah, Alice and Joe. You are everything.

This publication was supported using public funding by the National Lottery through Arts Council England.

Mantle Lane Press would like to acknowledge support from Writing West Midlands.

Mantle Lane Press is a subsidiary of Mantle Arts Limited, which receives financial support from North West Leicestershire District Council.